Little Lizzy and the Big Blue Parade

By Dr. Liz
Illustrated by Dustin Evans

Printed in the United States of America
Perfection Press

ISBN: 978-1-62920-982-1

Visit Little Lizzy online at:
www.littlelizzy.org

Thank you to the Rev. Dr. Kahli Mootoo for your friendship and spiritual guidance. Thank you Vicki, Nia, Karyn, Gina, Santia, Maxine, Danielle, Tesha, Kristy, Mona, Bill, Frances, Desiree, Anthony, and Tiffany for being part of the village that got me through this journey. I love you all.
—Dr. Liz

Lizzy couldn't believe it. "I won!" she said. It was the first time she had ever beaten her older brother, Neil, in a game of checkers.

All through dinner, Lizzy teased Neil about winning. She felt like she was on top of the world.

But then things changed. Lizzy's tummy started to hurt. She felt sick. Her mom gave her ginger tea, but it didn't help.

Over the next few days, Lizzy got worse. She had a fever. Her tummy hurt a lot.

Lizzy's mom could always make her feel better when she was sick. But not this time. Lizzy even drank that yucky pink stuff for bellyaches. Nothing helped.

Lizzy's fever wouldn't go away. Her mom called an ambulance. At the hospital, nurses gave Lizzy medicine called **antibiotics**. It dripped from a bag hanging from a pole.

antibiotic: a drug used to treat infections

Lizzy was in and out of the hospital for months. She wasn't getting any better. So Lizzy's mom took her to a different hospital. She saw a new doctor.

Lizzy stayed in the new hospital for days. After lots of tests, Dr. Rhee figured out what was wrong. Lizzy had cancer in her belly.

Lizzy had heard the word *cancer* before. But she didn't know what it meant. Dr. Rhee explained that cancer is a disease. It attacks the cells in a person's body. That's what made Lizzy's tummy feel bad.

Dr. Rhee said Lizzy would need surgery to remove the bad cells. After surgery, she would get a special medicine called **chemotherapy**. It would help make sure the cancer never came back.

chemotherapy: a type of medicine that uses chemicals to help treat cancer

Lizzy started chemotherapy the next week at the cancer center. She got medicine in her arm for four hours every week.

When Lizzy got chemo, she sat and read. She didn't want to fall behind in school. She asked the nurses to label all the things that were new to her. Lizzy even had the nurses record her reading books out loud so she could share them with her friends.

Lizzy felt sicker every week. She didn't understand how a medicine that was supposed to make her feel better made her feel worse. She had asked her mom if she could stop taking the chemotherapy. But her mom said she couldn't. The medicine made sure the cancer stayed out of her belly.

Lizzy had two best friends, Veda and Malissa. They came over every Friday with a grilled-cheese sandwich, Lizzy's favorite. They washed their hands, wore masks, and even put shoe covers over their shoes. This helped keep Lizzy safe. They had learned this routine from Lizzy's mom. She explained that chemo kills bad cells and good cells in a person's body. Lizzy could get sick very easily. She was ***immunocompromised***.

immunocompromised: unable to fight off illness due to a medical condition

14

Before Lizzy got cancer, the three friends would pretend to be the Supremes. Lizzy was Diana Ross, of course. She always sang the lead. After the girls ate their lunch, they would sing "Ain't No Mountain High Enough." They would always hug Lizzy when they got to the line that said "keep me from getting to you." This made Lizzy smile. She loved her friends.

When it was time to leave, Lizzy gave her friends a gift. It was hand sanitizer. Whenever anyone visited her, she would give them hand sanitizer and say, "Be wise and always sanitize."

Sometimes Lizzy would get sad about being sick with cancer. She would grab all of the "get-well" cards and letters people sent her. There were hundreds.

She spread them out on her bed. It made her feel better knowing so many people cared about her.

Lizzy was scared and cried all the time. She cried even more when the hair on the sides of her head started to fall out. But her mom cut off the sides completely and gave Lizzy a cool mohawk.

Then her mom planned a surprise haircut party. The whole neighborhood came out and shaved the sides of their heads too. Everyone had a mohawk like Lizzy's. People even gave money to help pay for her medicine. Lizzy felt pretty special.

A reporter, Mike, from the Daily Newspaper wrote about what Lizzy's neighbors and friends did. He called the article "Mohawk Town." He said Lizzy was brave and strong for working hard to beat cancer. He also praised her for keeping up with her schoolwork. He called Lizzy the Hometown Hero of Brooklyn.

citation: an award for an achievement

After 12 rounds of chemo, Lizzy was finished with her treatment. The doctors and nurses had a red carpet laid out for her to walk down to a special bell. Whenever anyone finishes cancer treatments, they ring a bell three times. The doctors and nurses gave Lizzy a small blue bell to take home. The Brooklyn Borough President even gave her a **citation**.

In a few weeks, Lizzy started to get her strength back. Soon, she was strong enough to return to school. Her teacher was surprised that Lizzy's reading skills were better than ever. Lizzy knew a lot of new words—mostly medical words!

Lizzy's birthday came six months later. Her family threw a huge celebration. It began with a big parade. The parade started a few blocks away from her home. It ended with a party at Lizzy's house on Crown Street. The party stretched the whole block. Friends from school, church, and the neighborhood came out to celebrate Lizzy's life and her beating cancer.

Lizzy's siblings, Neil and Michelle, helped decorate the block with balloons and streamers. They used shades of blue everywhere. People with Lizzy's type of cancer are honored with the color blue.

Lizzy made a speech to thank everyone. She said, "Today is a celebration for my birthday, but today I celebrate all of you. Your kindness saved my life. Your love was my medicine. Your love filled my bucket. Love is the most powerful thing, and we have so much of it here. I love you all!"